# VICTORY SCHOOL SUPERSTARS

STONE ARCH BOOKS
a capstone imprint

**Sports Illustrated KIDS**

# I Broke into Gymnastics Camp

by Jessica Gunderson
illustrated by Jorge Santillan

STONE ARCH BOOKS
a capstone imprint

Sports Illustrated KIDS *I Broke into Gymnastics Camp*
is published by Stone Arch Books — A Capstone Imprint
1710 Roe Crest Drive
North Mankato, Minnesota 56003
www.capstonepub.com

Art Director: Bob Lentz
Graphic Designer: Hilary Wacholz
Production Specialist: Michelle Biedscheid

Timeline photo credits: Shutterstock/Pavel Mikushin (top left);
Sports Illustrated/Al Tielemans (bottom left), Robert Beck,
(middle & bottom right); Wikipedia, (top right).

Printed in the United States of America in Stevens Point,
Wisconsin.
102011
006404WZS12

Library of Congress Cataloging-in-Publication Data
Gunderson, Jessica.
   I broke into gymnastics camp / by Jessica Gunderson; illustrated by
Jorge H. Santillan.
      p. cm. — (Sports illustrated kids. Victory School superstars)
   Summary: Kenzie is so excited by the first day of gymnastics camp that
she accidentally breaks the lock on the gym door—will she confess to the
damage or let camp be canceled for everybody?
   ISBN 978-1-4342-2245-9 (library binding)
   ISBN 978-1-4342-3869-6 (pbk.)
   1. Gymnastics—Juvenile fiction. 2. Honesty—Juvenile fiction.
[1. Gymnastics—Fiction. 2. Honesty—Fiction. 3. Camps—Fiction.]
I. Santillan, Jorge, ill. II. Title. III. Series: Sports Illustrated kids. Victory
School superstars.
   PZ7.G963Iag 2012
   813.6—dc23                                    2011032819

# TABLE of CONTENTS

# KENZIE WINZ

**Gymnastics**

AGE: 10
GRADE: 4
SUPER SPORTS ABILITY: Super strength

## VICTORY SCHOOL SUPERSTARS

**CARMEN**

**DANNY**

**ALICIA**

**TYLER**

**JOSH**

# VICTORY SCHOOL MAP

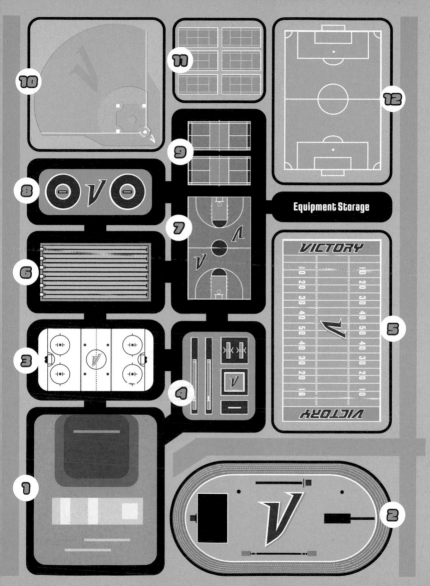

Equipment Storage

1. BMX/Skateboarding
2. Track and Field
3. Hockey/Figure Skating
4. Gymnastics
5. Football
6. Swimming
7. Basketball
8. Wrestling
9. Volleyball
10. Baseball/Softball
11. Tennis
12. Soccer

# First Day of Camp

Today is going to be the best day ever. It's the day I've been waiting for all summer — the first day of gymnastics camp.

Our school van pulls up in front of the camp gym.

"We're here!" I shout, pulling open the door and jumping out.

"Wait for us, Kenzie!" my friends Wendy and Alicia yell from behind me.

I don't wait, though. I keep running toward the gym door. But Alicia still beats me there, leaping ahead of me at the last moment.

"Locked!" she says, pulling on the door handle.

"What?" I exclaim, unable to wait any longer. "Let me try!"

I push Alicia aside with my fingertip, grab the handle, and pull with all my might.

*SNAP!* The lock shatters, and the door nearly flies off its hinges.

"Oops," I say. I'm surprised by my own strength, even though this kind of thing happens all the time.

How did I do it? You see, I have super strength. I am stronger than anyone I know. Even the adults.

"You broke the lock," Wendy whispers.

I shrug. "I break things all the time," I say. I act like it's no big deal, but inside I am worried that I will get in trouble on the first day of camp.

"What are you going to do?" Wendy asks.

"What are you going to do about what?" says a voice behind us.

We turn. A young woman stands behind us, wearing a purple gym suit. But she's not just any woman.

I can't believe my eyes. I blink. I must be imagining her. But no. She's real.

"Emmy Winter!" I exclaim.

Who's Emmy Winter? She's only the very best gymnast in the whole entire world. At least I think so. I watch her every time she's on TV. I even have a poster of her on my bedroom wall.

"I didn't know you were going to be here!" I say with a gasp.

"It was meant to be a surprise," Emmy says. "But you girls are early."

I let go of the open door, hoping Emmy won't notice. But she does.

She brushes past me and pulls on the door. "That's strange," she says. "The gym was supposed to be locked."

Wendy and Alicia glare at me. My face burns. I know I should tell Emmy what I've done. But I can't. I just can't.

# CHAPTER 2

# Surprise Spoiler

Wendy and Alicia keep glaring at me as Emmy hurries toward the gym office.

"What?" I say, glaring back. "You don't know what it's like to have super strength."

That's not true, not really. All three of us attend Victory School for Super Athletes, where each student has a special athletic ability.

Alicia has a super jumping ability, which helps her in her favorite sport of cheerleading. Wendy, or "Bendy Wendy," as everyone calls her, has super flexibility.

"Yeah, but we don't use our special skills to our advantage," Wendy argues.

"And we admit it if we accidentally break something because of our skill," Alicia adds. "Like the time I jumped and broke the light in the hallway. I could have kept it a secret, but that wouldn't have been right."

"You're ruining my favorite day ever,"
I groan. "Let's go warm up."

Soon the gym is full of other kids — boys
on one side and girls on the other. I've
forgotten all about the broken lock. I just
can't wait to start tumbling.

I say hello to a group of girls who sit down next to us. I never used to like meeting new people. Then last year on our school trip to Triumph Mountain, I met a girl from Hawaii. We became great friends. Maybe I'll make another friend this week.

"Did you know that Emmy Winter is going to be here?" I suddenly blurt out.

The girls' eyes widen. "Emmy Winter!" they exclaim.

Alicia nudges me. "That's supposed to be a surprise, Kenzie," she says. "I guess your super strength isn't the only thing that's hard to control."

I want to take back the secret, but I can't. The word has spread throughout the gym. Everyone is whispering about Emmy.

Just then, the head coach, Deb, enters the gym and greets us. I sigh with relief as everyone stops talking and listens.

Coach Deb starts introducing herself. Then suddenly, somebody shouts, "Where's Emmy?"

Coach Deb's face reddens. My heart falls with a bang.

Emmy strides in. She looks a little angry. *Maybe that's how she always looks,* I think.

"Surprise, everyone!" she says. I can tell by her tone that she knows the surprise has been ruined. She looks straight toward me, her eyes burning, and I look down at the floor.

# The Back Handspring

As the day goes on, I barely watch as the coaches perform for us. But my eyes are glued to Emmy when it is her turn. She is the star tumbler, of course.

I am amazed as she zigs and zags across the mat. She does a string of aerial cartwheels that make her look like a pinwheel.

She ends her performance with a trio of back handsprings. She sticks her landing every time.

"She's great. It's no wonder you love her, Kenzie!" says Alicia. She doesn't sound mad anymore. I relax. Maybe Emmy has forgotten all about it, too.

Moments later, we are divided into groups according to our best event. Bendy Wendy rushes toward the balance beam, and Alicia heads to the uneven bars.

I, of course, stay close to the spring floor, where we will practice tumbling.

My heart triples its speed when I see that Emmy is the coach for my group. I can't wait to show her what I can do. I can't wait to show her how good I am.

Emmy shows us a back handspring. "Remember to push hard off the hands," she says. "And keep the arms straight and strong."

I am only half-listening. I've known how to do a back handspring for years. Instead, I'm thinking about how amazing it will be for Emmy to see what I can do.

Maybe she will want me to be on her team. Maybe I will be able to quit school and tour around the world with Emmy instead.

"Next!" calls Emmy. I realize it's my turn. My face burns. I haven't been paying attention. I'm not ready.

She is staring at me. "Oh. It's you," she says.

I walk onto the mat. My knees are shaking. And as you might know, it is not easy to do a back handspring when your knees are knocking together.

But I do one anyway.

A bad one.

I don't control my strength when I push from my hands. I fly wildly into the air. My landing is hard and wobbly. My feet slide across the mat as though it's made of ice.

"Whoa," Emmy says. She reaches out a hand to steady me. "You need to work on your control."

"I go to Victory Sports School," I begin.

I want to explain why my landing is so
terrible.

But she looks at me blankly. "Next!" she
calls.

Discovery

I turn away, tears in my eyes.
Gymnastics camp isn't turning out like I
wanted it to. Not at all! I wish I could start
the day over. I wouldn't break the lock. I
wouldn't tell anyone about Emmy. And
I wouldn't daydream. Then maybe I'd at
least be enjoying the camp.

The next girl in line, Liz, steps up to the mat. She completes a perfect back handspring. And she lands without a wobble.

Emmy beams at the girl. "Excellent!" she says, clapping.

I would give anything to be Liz right now. I would even give up my super strength.

I watch as each of the girls performs a back handspring. Each of them does better than I did. Pretty soon, I can't even see through the thick tears that fill my eyes.

"Time for a break," Emmy says. As I turn toward the bleachers, I feel a tap on my shoulder.

It's Emmy. "Kenzie, may I speak with you?" she says. "I want to tell you that I think you're—"

She's interrupted by a loud shout. Coach Deb is striding quickly into the gym. "Listen up, everybody!" she says. "I don't want to cause alarm, but someone has broken into the gym."

I try to look relaxed, in spite of my reddening face.

Coach Deb goes on. "For your safety, the camp is cancelled for the rest of the day. Return to your rooms until further notice."

Everyone groans. Alicia and Wendy whip their heads to look at me.

"Wait!" I call to the coach. But she doesn't hear me above everyone's groans. "Wait!" I yell again, pushing through the other students.

I have to tell the truth. Even if I'm punished. Even if I'm sent home.

# Telling the Truth

I am breathless when I reach the coach. Emmy is right behind me.

"It was me!" I gasp. "I broke the lock!"

The coach stares hard at me, and then whistles loudly. The gym falls silent.

Everyone is listening.

"What?" the coach asks.

"I broke the lock," I repeat. I stare down at the floor, hoping that somehow it will open up and swallow me.

Coach Deb frowns. "You? How could you break the lock?"

"I have super strength," I mumble.

Coach Deb glares. "If this is true, you'll have to be punished. And if it's not true, then you'll be punished for lying."

"It's true," says a voice behind me. I turn and see Alicia coming toward us, with Wendy at her heels.

"We saw it happen," says Alicia. "We should have told. If Kenzie gets in trouble, so should we."

"I didn't mean to do it," I add. "I was just so excited."

"Accidents happen," Coach says. "But it wasn't right that you didn't report it. Maybe you should sit out the rest of the day."

Then Emmy steps forward. "I think you should let Kenzie stay," she says. "I'd love to keep working with her. She has amazing talent. She just needs to control herself better. I can help her."

I stare at Emmy, who smiles back at me. I can't believe my ears. It's like a dream come true.

Coach sighs. "Let's take a snack break," she says. "And I'll think about it."

As Coach walks away, Emmy winks at me. "I think she'll let you stay," she says. "But you'll have to work extra hard to keep those amazing skills under control."

"I will," I say. "And I'm sorry that I spoiled your surprise."

Emmy laughs. "You remind me of myself when I was your age. I could never keep secrets either," she says. "Now let's go eat."

I smile and skip toward the lunch room. Today may not be the very best day ever, but it's close.

# GLOSSARY

**ability** (uh-BIL-i-tee)—skill or power

**aerial cartwheel** (AIR-ee-uhl KART-weel)—a cartwheel done without touching hands to the ground

**accidentally** (AK-si-dehn-tuh-lee)—done by chance or without trying to

**balance beam** (BAL-uhnss BEEM)—a narrow beam used in gymnastics, usually four feet off the floor

**flexibility** (flek-suh-BIL-uh-tee)—the ability to bend

**glaring** (GLAIR-ing)—looking at someone in an angry way

**handsprings** (HAND-springz)—stunts in which you spring forward or backward onto both hands, then flip all the way over to land on your feet

**punished** (PUHN-ishd)—made someone suffer for behaving badly

**uneven bars** (uhn-EE-vuhn BARS)—a piece of gymnastics equipment made of a steel frame and a set of bars that are placed at different heights

# JESSICA GUNDERSON

Jessica Gunderson grew up in North Dakota. She took gymnastics classes when she was little and remembers being scared of the balance beam and high bars. Gymnastics is her favorite Olympic sport to watch. Jessica currently lives in Madison, Wisconsin, with her husband. She has a cat who thinks he is a gymnast, but he's big and clumsy and sometimes falls when he's jumping.

# JORGE SANTILLAN

Jorge Santillan got his start illustrating in the children's sections of local newspapers. He opened his own illustration studio in 2005. His creative team specializes in books, comics, and children's magazines. Jorge lives in Mendoza, Argentina, with his wife, Bety; son, Luca; and their four dogs, Fito, Caro, Angie, and Sammy.

# GYMNASTICS IN HISTORY

**2500 B.C.**
A **live bull** is used in a gymnastics event in ancient Greece.

**1811 A.D.**
The first gymnastics center opens near Berlin, Germany.

**1928**
Women gymnasts compete in the Olympics for the first time.

**1970**
Cathy Rigby wins a silver medal at the world championships. She is the first American to win a world medal in gymnastics.

**1976**
**Nadia Comaneci** from Romania scores the first perfect 10 in Olympic history.

**1984**
American **Mary Lou Retton** wins top all-around gymnast at the Olympics. *Sports Illustrated* names her Sportswoman of the Year.

**1996**
The **U.S. women's team** wins the team gold medal at the Olympics. They are nicknamed the "Magnificent Seven."

**2006**
Gymnastic scoring is changed. Gymnasts can no longer earn a **perfect 10** Some gymnasts and coaches do not like the new system.

**2010**
China's Winter Olympics snowboarding team includes former gymnasts.

# Kenzie Winz
## Comes Out on Top!

If you liked *Kenzie's* gymnastics adventure, check out her other *sports stories*.

# Don't Break the Balance Beam!

Kenzie's super strength makes her a super tumbler. But when she doesn't control her strength on the beam, it's a disaster. Now all of her teammates are laughing and saying one thing: don't break the balance beam!

# I Just Have to Ride the Halfpipe!

Kenzie's ski lesson left her in a heap in the snow. But a new friend shows her the perfect snow sport for her gymnastic skills — snowboarding. All she's thinking now is, "I just have to ride the halfpipe!"

# There's a Hurricane in the Pool!

Kenzie hates swimming in gym class. She tried to control her strength during her laps, but then she falls behind everyone. When she lets loose, her kicks cause huge waves. Before she knows what's happening, there's a hurricane in the pool!

STONE ARCH BOOKS
a capstone imprint